The First Hunter

by

Robert Swindells

First published in 2009 in Great Britain by
Barrington Stoke Ltd
18 Walker Street, Edinburgh, EH3 7LP

www.barringtonstoke.co.uk

ISBN: 978-1-84299-698-0

Printed in Great Britain by Bell & Bain Ltd

A Note from the Author

How did early humans get their meat? Did they start hunting animals to eat when they learnt how to make good weapons? That's what scientists and historians always thought. No one ever thought that for a while early humans were like jackals and hyenas – that they stole meat from big cats because they couldn't hunt for themselves.

Then we invented the electron microscope. Everything we'd thought about early humans changed. Scientists looked at the animal bones that had been found at prehistoric sites again – with the new microscope. They saw the bones had lots of different marks on them. Some were marks made by flint knives and blades the humans had used to cut and scrape the meat from the bones. But there were other marks too – underneath the ones the humans had made. These were fang and claw marks made by large predators. The animals whose bones these were, had been killed by big cats, not by humans. The human hunters had just taken the bones from the big cats and then cut away the meat to eat.

The First Hunter is the story of how I think humans stole the big cats' meat, and then how all that changed when they started to hunt for themselves.

For Martin and Sinead Kromer,
without whose tireless work with the
Federation of Children's Book Groups,
countless young people might never have
encountered a great number of
brilliant books.

Contents

Chapter 1
Prints in the Dew

My name is Tan. I snatch meat from big cats' kills. I'm Tan the snatcher and I'm fast. I have to be.

Our place under the cliff is deep and dry. We sleep here, behind our fire. Dip works with me. He has the fire that scares off the cats. He scares them off their kills, so I can snatch the meat. I'm fast, but he's brave.

I'm the Snatcher. Dip is the Brand-man. The stick with the fire is called a brand. Dip waves the brand to scare the cats.

So that's Dip and me. Then there's Gak and Lom who carry the meat home and Sil and Mab who are the mothers. Dol is the Old One and there are four Little Ones. Last of all is Wid, the Fool. We all live togther in our place under the cliff.

Wid the Fool looks after the Little Ones so that Sil and Mab can hunt for mice and frogs, eggs and honey. Wid's head is full of feathers and fur but he's my friend. Dol is Mother to us both.

It is morning. The grass is wet, but the sun is coming. I get up from under the cliff and look downhill to the grass-land. In the night we heard a lion kill a zebra. Now the lion has that meat, his kill. He's watching the meat somewhere safe and secret. Maybe under a clump of trees. I can't see the kill but my nose can smell it.

"Tan," Dip calls to me. He comes out from under the cliff and stretches. "Are you ready?"

I nod. "Ready and hungry, Dip. Is Gak awake?"

"He's coming now. Have you got your knife?"

"Of course." I show him the sharp blade of flint. "And you – have you got the brand?"

Dip stoops and pulls a stick from the fire. It's still hot. I can see its smoke. "Right here," Dip says, and holds the smoking stick up high.

A Little One gets up too and comes over to us. His name is Bub. He rubs his eyes. "Can I come with you, Tan? I'm fast and strong."

"Fast *and* strong," I laugh. "You'll be a Brand-man *and* a Snatcher, Bub." I muss his hair. "But not today, eh? One more winter, then we'll see."

Bub goes grumbling back to the shelter as Gak comes out. The three of us start downhill, leaving our foot prints in the dew.

The grass is long and yellow, like the lion. He's hard to see. "There." I point. "In the tree-shadow," I whisper. Dip nods. "I see him. I see his kill too, four steps to his left. It's a zebra." The kill has stripes, like the shadow.

Dip bends down and pulls up some long dry grass. Gak and I watch the lion, who is sleeping, full of meat. Dip winds the grass round and round the smoking stick to make his brand. "Ready?" he whispers. I nod. Gak nods.

Dip puts his mouth near to the brand and blows. The stick glows. The grass crackles. Flames leap. Dip runs at the lion. He screams and waves the brand over his head. The lion wakes, lifts his head and snarls. His mane is like the flames. The lion stands, ready to charge, but then he sees the fire. He backs off, growling. Stands over his kill.

Dip is brave, he doesn't stop. He runs at the great cat. The stick is high over his head and ablaze with fire. The lion roars. This is the worst part. Sometimes a lion will charge the fire, kill the Brand-man with one slash of its terrible claws. Most times it will turn and bound away, but not very far.

This cat turns, trots into thorn bush and looks back at us. It wants the kill. Dip follows the lion to drive it a little farther away. Now it's my turn. I run to the zebra, slash open its skin with my knife and cut deep. "Quick!" warns Dip, "soon he'll charge the flames."

I'm working as fast as I can. Zebra flesh is tough, stringy. The meat won't come away. Then Gak is beside me. He grips the hoof and pulls. He's strong – he tears the leg from the zebra's body, heaves it onto his back and trots away. It's as if it's the leg of a mouse – not the heavy leg of a zebra.

"All clear, Dip!" I leap up, run after Gak the Carrier. I don't look back, but I know Dip will back off slowly. He'll keep on waving his brand until he's with us. And when the lion sees

5

what's left of the kill, still under the trees, it will lose interest in Dip. If he's lucky. Brand-men need luck and courage. Dip has both.

Gak walks uphill like a man carrying nothing. The others have seen him coming, seen the meat, seen Dip and me and no lion. They dance in front of the cliff where we can see them. They're laughing and singing. We're all hungry, our mouths water as we think of the feast we'll have.

This time, it's only the zebra that's died.

Chapter 2
Jackal Dance

The meat is on a spit over the fire. It smells good. We'll do the Lion Dance while it cooks, then eat till every belly is tight.

Gak is the lion. He wears a lion skin. Its head is on his head. The lion is sleeping. The Little Ones sit nearby. They are mice and birds and lizards. They whistle and wiggle their fingers. The lion does not wake.

Wid is the kill. He lies still. He has a zebra skin over him.

Lom and me and Sil and Mab are Brand-men and Snatchers. We creep towards the sleeping lion. Dol the Old One sings softly a sad song – a song of empty bellies.

We are near the lion now. The mice and birds and lizards have heard us, seen us. Their whistles grow louder, their fingers faster. They are waking the lion. Dol's song is louder too – and now her song makes our hearts thump. We hold our breath.

The lion lifts his head. Now is the time. Now. Sil and Mab, me and Lom stop creeping, start running. We scream and flap our arms as we charge at the cat. Dol's song is loud and high. She rocks herself, screeches out her song and clashes two stones together.

The lion is up and snarling. He shows teeth and claws, he guards his kill. The four of us run at him. The Little Ones squeal and bounce and wiggle. They are so excited that they've forgotten to be mice and birds and lizards.

The lion turns and bounds away. We close round the kill, pull off the skin, pretend to cut meat off the zebra. Now Wid curls up in the middle of us and puts his arms round his head. He laughs. The Little Ones shove in and paw Wid's body. Dol's song ends with a shout of joy.

The Lion Dance is over. We stand still as we pant and grin and smell the meat we've won for a second time.

We sit in a circle round the cooked meat to eat it. Everyone is there except Lom. He's taken his meat and his spear to the hilltop. There are many dangerous animals, even in the daytime. Someone must always watch.

Wid is next to me. "Poor zebra," he moans and he strokes his chunk of meat. "Poor zebra."

I look at him. "Dip won that meat for you, Wid, but I'll have it if you don't want it – you can have a frog or some roots. Give it here." I hold out my hand.

"*No!*" He sways away from me, and holds the meat tight. Then he turns back to me and says, "Dip *didn't* win this meat. Lion won it. Us like jackals. We *steal* meat. Our dance is a *jackal* dance. More better we *lion*, not jackal." He starts to cry.

The Little Ones nudge one another and giggle. I frown at them and they stop. I put an arm round Wid.

"Dip made the lion run off, Wid. That was very brave. He won the meat for you."

"We *all* won it," growls Gak.

Ever since Wid's body grew up and his brain did not, most of the others have wanted to move on and leave him behind, to be eaten by wolves or cats. *Why should we face danger to get food for him?* they ask. *He's no use.* But

Dol and I won't let them leave Wid behind for wolves and cats to kill. We keep him safe.

It's lucky we've eaten well. Everyone hears Wid call us jackals but they're sleepy and full. They think, *who cares what Wid the Fool says? He's got feathers and fur for brains.*

That night it's my turn to keep watch, feed the fire. It's a still night with a clear sky and a moon as fat as our bellies. The moon floods the grass-land with silver. I sit on a stone, my spear across my knees.

Wid the Fool, I think. *Most of the time his talk is like the chatter of rooks. But not tonight.* More better we lion, not jackal, *he said. He's right. But how can we get meat? We have no claws, no fangs and we're weak and small. How can we be lions?*

Soon a wind springs up. It lifts sparks from the fire and blows them at the moon, which rolls on towards the dawn.

Chapter 3

Bear

In the daylight I can see scraps of meat on the ground. Roots and berries too. We gather it all into one pile.   There's enough food for all of us, for today. No need to hunt or search. We can stay by the cliff and be safe.

This is what I think, after I've been on watch all night. My head is fuzzy, I should know no place is safe.

I am sleeping by the fire when Bub the Little One cries out. "Bear!" he shouts. "Bear, bear, bear!"

I lift my head. It is still fuzzy. Bub is jumping up and down on the stone I sat on last night. "Shush, Bub," I snarl. "It's too early for your games."

Mab gets up. She is Bub's mother. She looks where Bub is pointing, then at me. "It's no game, Tan. There's a bear – a big one. And it's coming this way."

I jump up and grab my spear. Of all beasts, the bear is the most dangerous to us. This is because we live in caves and by cliffs, and the bear does too. Sometimes, our home has been a bear's home before we came, and we don't know it. The bear comes back and attacks to drive us away. Also, bears don't see very well. In the daytime they can't see our fires. So they aren't scared of us.

I think I know why this bear has come. He can smell last night's feast. His eyes may be dim, but he has a keen nose. He may have followed it all night.

We all stand together at the top of the hill. We're all there, even Wid the Fool. We shout and scream at the top of our lungs. We bang stones together, beat the earth with sticks and wave our arms. Sometimes, if you make a lot of noise, the bear will turn away. He can't see what's making all the noise – he hears it and sees something move. *Is it a monster?* he thinks.

It doesn't work. The bear stops and swings his huge head from side to side. He sniffs the wind. There's noise, but he can smell food, and the food wins. He drops his head and comes loping up towards us.

"Dol!" I rap. "Take the Little Ones to the top of the cliff. Wid, go with them. If the bear gets us, run. Don't stop, don't look back."

Now there are six of us. Six spears, one bear. Our chances sound good, but they're not. A bear's fur is thick. Too thick for flint points.

Ram a spear into that fur and it will snap.
Hurl the spear and it will bounce off.

There is only one place to hit the bear – the
bear's mouth. The mouth must be open and
you must hit hard and fast. The point must go
into the mouth before the beast can close its
teeth and snap the spear. You have to hurl
yourself forward to get all the force you need.
And if your strike fails, the bear's great arms
will pull you in and you'll die.

The six of us stand with our spears pointed
at the beast. We'll have to fool him – that way
he won't know which of us to charge first. We
fan out, we dance on our toes and jab at him
as he comes close. Soon there's blood on the
bear's nose.

The bear gets angry. He rears up on his
back legs. He's taller than Lom, and Lom is
tall. He roars and roars and slashes at our
spears with long claws like hooks. We take
turns to skip at him, jab him and skip back.

The blood mixes with the foam around his mouth and turns it pink. We hope the bear will give up and turn away, but he doesn't. He's hungry for meat, and he wants us dead.

Suddenly it happens. Dip skips too close, stays too long. A great paw lashes out at him and cuts open his chest from neck to hip. Dip cries out and falls, leaving his spear in the bear's jaws. The bear roars and bats at the spear with its paws. Pink foam flies from its open mouth.

Mab sees her chance. With a shout she dives at the bear and drives her spear into its mouth. It goes deep. The bear shakes its head with panic and hurls Mab to the ground. She rolls away and the bear comes down on all fours again. It's shaking its head to try to be rid of the two spears.

At last the bear has had enough. It turns and shambles away down the slope. We can see the spears sticking out of its mouth like tusks. They catch on bushes and rocks as the bear moves off.

Dol and the others have seen our victory. They come down with shouts and whoops of joy. The shouting dies away when they see Dip lying on the ground. Gak and Lom carry him back to our place under the cliff. They put him to lie on furs. Dol brings plants to rub where his chest is ripped open. Sometimes a man will survive a bear attack like his.

Sometimes.

Chapter 4

Until We Meet Again

Dip lies close to the fire. We feed the fire to keep it bright and strong. We pack his cuts with herbs, but one night the darkness gets into Dip. It leaves its stinking blackness in his cuts. Dip is brave, but that's not enough. You can't run at the blackness with a brand. Nothing will drive it away. The blackness melts Dip's flesh and turns it to maggots, which eat him.

Dip takes many days to die. His pain is great, but he never cries out. Dol is with him at the end. When we come back to the cliff with honey, eggs and roots one day, he is gone. Dol has laid the lion skin over him. The Little Ones sit silent for once. No one moves. Wid slumps nearby. His moon-face is wet with tears.

We carry Dip away from our cliff to the leaving place. Dol sings. Her song tells how his spirit will follow the sun far to the west, where animals only eat grass and it is always day.

Fare well, Dip the Brand-man. Until we meet again.

****

"No Brand-man, no meat." Mab the Mother says this as we sit round the fire that night, thinking about our friend.

"Long ago," says Dol, "the people had no meat. They lived on small things – roots, mice, berries, things like that. We can do this."

"We don't have to," pipes Bub the Little One. Mab frowns at him. She is his mother. Little Ones do not speak out. I smile at him. "You are brave enough to be our new Brandman, Bub, but not big enough. I told you – one more winter."

The child slumps and stares into the flames. Mab looks at me. "I can fill Dip's place till Bub is grown."

"*You*, Mab?" I ask. A child does not speak out. A woman does not carry the brand. She nods. "I drove away the bear, didn't I?"

I nod and look at Dol. "What d'you think, Old One?" The old woman gives a shrug. "There was a Brand-woman when I was a Little One. Lidi was her name. She scared off many a lion." Dol smiles. "And a man or two, if I remember."

"What happened to her, Old One?" Bub asks.

Dol sighs. "Sabre-tooth tiger got her, Bub. We don't see sabre-tooths any more, and that's good. You had to be very brave to run at a sabre-tooth."

We all agree. When I snatch again, Mab will be Brand-woman.

Next day we don't look for meat. We are sad after Dip's death. We feel slow, not hungry. Dol says, "I can't help you with this, but the bees can."

She means honey. Honey will make a slow man fast. Rotten honey will make a sad man laugh. Sil and Mab know where to go. "There's a tree," says Mab. "A tall dead hollow tree, in the middle of the forest. Bees make nests there – a new nest every spring. There are old nests full of rotten honey – enough for us all."

We all go except Dol. She can't walk that far. The Little Ones are excited. They want to run ahead, but we do not let them. "There are lions," warns Lom, "and bears and snakes and leopards. Stay close." They walk near Lom and Gak, and look into the woods with big eyes.

We find the hollow tree. I look up. Near the top is a hole and a cloud of bees. They would sting me to death, but Sil and Mab know what to do. Mab has a stick from the fire. She plucks handfuls of grass. Not dry grass like a Brand-man, but damp green grass. She winds this round her stick, and blows on the end. No flame comes, only thick white smoke. Sil has put a rabbit-skin over her head. It has holes for her eyes and mouth. She goes up the tree, fast as a squirrel. Mab goes after her. We stand underneath, looking up.

At the top, Mab waves the smoking stick in the cloud of bees. Sil sticks her arm into the hole. She must be getting stung, but she takes no notice. She feels about and breaks off lumps of honey-comb and drops them at our feet. The smoke is making the bees sleepy. Most of them don't attack the women, but I'm glad I'm not up there.

Soon, there is a great pile of honey-comb on the ground. It shines, packed with honey. Sil and Mab climb down. Sil's arm is full of stings, but she doesn't care. We sit under the tree, fill our fists with honey and cram it into our mouths. The honey is so rotten, it makes us drunk. We laugh as Wid and the Little Ones fall down, shouting and giggling. Only Lom doesn't eat. He stands with his spear and keeps watch for danger.

When we've eaten all we can, we put what's left into a wolf skin for Lom and Dol. Then we weave our way back to the overhang. We haven't forgotten Dip, but we know he's happy, so we're happy for him.

Wise woman, old Dol.

Chapter 5
Wid's Game

A storm comes in the night. The sky
throws down spears to stab us, and roars when
they miss. Rain drums on the earth and drops
sheets of water so close to our shelter that Dol
has to shift the fire. Wid is afraid of storms
and crawls under my heap of skins. I hold him.

Day dawns misty. The sun is a pale, fuzzy
ball. Our heads are fuzzy too, from the honey.
Everyone is thirsty. We troop to the river,
dunk our heads in the icy water and suck.

Now we're hungry. I look at Mab. "Pick
your brand from the fire, Mab – it is time."

We set off downhill and leave Dol to tend the fire and Wid to watch the Little Ones. I am thinking two things – *will Mab protect me when I cut up the kill?* Then I think, *Wid is right – we get our meat like jackals.* I don't like this second thought.

We walk out onto the plain. The sun is drying the ground and burning off the mist. We use our eyes, ears and noses to look for a cat that killed in the storm.

After a long time Gak stops and holds up a hand. "A fresh kill lies close by," he whispers. He nods towards a stand of tall grass. "In there."

Mab bends down to pick some grass for her brand. The sun has dried it just in time. We all look towards the tall grass. Sil looks at Gak. "What sort of cat is it?"

Gak shakes his head. "I can't tell, Sil. Even *my* nose can't work it out ..." he says softly.

"Is it a sabre-tooth?"

Gak shakes his head. "No sabre-tooths left," he murmurs. "I hope."

Mab stands up, blows on her brand. She must be afraid, but does not show it. "Ready, Tan?" she whispers.

I nod. "Ready." We can't see what we're hunting. That's not good, but sometimes it has to be like this.

Mab fills her lungs, lets out a terrible screech and runs right into the long grass, with her brand high above her head. I'm at her heels, knife in hand.

Nothing happens at first. Could Gak have made a mistake? Maybe there isn't a cat here – and no kill? Mab is three steps from the tall grass when there's a crackling sound. The grass sways and a leopard breaks cover and bounds away with a snarl of anger and fear. Mab crashes right into the stand of grass, jumps over the body of a deer and drives the angry cat farther away. I crouch by the kill and slash through the skin and muscle to cut out the meat.

The leopard turns back to us, growling. Mab runs at it, but it doesn't move back. She stops, waves her brand, calls to me. "Hurry, Tan – she's coming back!"

I rip the meat free as Mab walks backwards towards me again. She is trying not to stumble. Her brand has burned down, there is only smoke. Lom seizes the meat and runs with it. Gak and Sil stand on both sides of Mab, spears ready. The cat comes on, showing us its fangs. We might kill it between us, but it's so close, it will rip someone's belly out first.

Then Mab does something none of us has ever seen before. She blows on her brand and swishes it through the long dry grass. Flames leap and crackle. The cat stops and turns aside. The four of us make our way through the smoke, coughing. Once we're out of the smoke and fire we run. The leopard does not follow.

When we get back to the cliff, Wid grabs my arm. The Little Ones grin up at me, excited. It isn't the meat, it's something they've been doing while we were away.

"Come," cries Wid. "See our game."

I'm hot, tired and hungry. I don't want to see a game. Wid makes up games for the Little Ones. He uses things he finds – stones, insects, bits of wood. Anything. It doesn't take much to keep the Little Ones happy.

But it's no use. Wid won't let me be. I have to go and see his game. I sigh and let him show me.

Wid has put some pale stones on the ground. And he's found a fishing stick. A fishing stick is a stick with a thin strip of hide tied to one end. You tie a bit of meat to the loose end of the strip and lower it into the river. Sometimes a fish will take the meat. If you're quick you can pull him out of the water before he sees what's going to happen and spits out the meat. You have to be very quick – better most times to eat the bit of meat yourself!

For this new game, Wid has stretched the strip and tied the free end to the other end of the fishing stick: the end you'd hold if you were fishing. The strip lies tightly against the stick now. Nothing hangs down. Wid has made something new. He grins and shows it to me. I can see he's very proud of it. "Very good, Wid," I tell him. "What's the game?"

"I do it, show you." He's got a little stack of thin, straight sticks. He picks one up, puts its thick end to the middle of the thong and stretches the thong. The fishing stick bends. He points the stick at the ring of stones and lets go of the thong. The stick flies a short way and falls into the ring. The Little Ones jump and shout. Wid grins. "Bub is best," he says. "He can put three sticks in the ring."

"Good, Wid." I nod. Good game." He holds out the stick. "Tan do it. Better than Bub, maybe."

I shake my head. "Not now, Wid. Bring the Little Ones to the fire. There's meat."

Good game. Maybe it's me who's the fool. Or maybe I'm just too tired and hungry to think.

Chapter 6

While We Sleep

The sun has gone west, to shine on Dip. We lie under the cliff, full of meat. We're happy. Mab is a brave Brand-woman, we won't go hungry.

I sleep, but my spirit does not. It stands looking at Wid's ring of stones. In its hand is the thing the Fool made from a fishing stick. *Tan do it*, says Wid, but he isn't there. Such things can happen where spirits go at night. My spirit lifts the stick. It is not a fishing stick now. It's long and smooth, like a tall pole. Wid's sticks lie on the ground. My spirit picks one up and fits it to the thong. The thong stretches. The tall pole bends. My spirit points the stick at the ring of stones and lets go. The stick flies, but it misses the ring. Wid and the Little Ones laugh, but they are not there.

The stick flies on till it hits a tree and bounces off. Dip is standing by the tree. He picks up the stick, smiles at my spirit. *If it had a point,* he calls, *it would not bounce off.*

I wake then, and for a moment I think it's real. "Dip!" I cry. "You have come back."

"Hush!" hisses Dol, from her place by the fire. "You'll scare the Little Ones, Tan."

"Dip," I mutter. "He's back, he was talking to me."

Dol shakes her head. "His spirit was talking to your spirit, Tan. No one comes back. Go to sleep."

We see all sorts of things when we sleep, but they melt in the morning like mist. This one did not. It was in my head when I woke up, and it was still there when I'd washed in the river.

It is a day to go and collect small food. Roots, eggs, lizards. I say, "There's a thing I must do today, here. Can you find food without me – for once?"

I watch Mab, Gak, Lom and Sil go off with baskets and spears. Wid is excited. He dances round me. He keeps saying, "The game, Tan. Play the game with us, ha?"

"Later, Wid," I tell him. "First I must cut a tall pole."

The Fool leads the Little Ones to his ring of stones. I look among the trees till I find one with long, straight branches. I cut one and trim it, so that it looks like the pole my spirit held in his hand last night. I take it to Dol.

"Have you got a thong as long as this?"
I ask. She looks at the long, springy pole.
"I have a strip of ox skin that's as long," she
tells me. "I was keeping it to sew two big skins
together to make a shelter from the wind."
She frowns. "What do you want it for, Tan?"

I smile. "Make Wid's game better, I hope,"
I tell her.

Dol doesn't want to give up the thong just
for a game but in the end she hands it to me.
I sit on a stone and cut a deep slot near each
end of my pole. I tie the ends of the thong into
both slots. Now the thong lies tight against
the pole. When I hook my finger round the
middle of the thong and pull it away from the
pole, the pole bends. My arm trembles from
the power that's in that bend.

Wid and three of the Little Ones are
laughing and shouting. They're playing their
game. Bub isn't playing. He stands on a rock

with his spear and keeps watch. "What's Tan got?" Wid asks.

"This?" I look at the thing I have made. "This is a Wid-thing and a spirit-thing," I tell him. "Watch."

I take one of the long, straight sticks. I fit it to the thong. Pull back with all my strength to bend the wand. When I let go, the stick flies over the ring, hits a tree and bounces off.

"Missed!" shouts Wid with a big happy grin.

"Missed!" cry the Little Ones and they jump and jig up and down.

Bub calls from his rock. "If it had a point, it wouldn't bounce off."

I stare at him. "That's ... that's what *Dip* said," I croak. I feel cold, unreal. Is it me standing here, or my spirit? Am I still sleeping?

Bub stares back at me. "Dip? Did you say *Dip?*" he asks.

"Uh … no." I shake my head. "No, not Dip. Listen, Bub, can you find me a sharp bit of flint. A little one. I want to make something like a spear-head, but smaller. I want to tie the head to a stick. It won't bounce off. It'll stick in the tree when I let it fly."

Chapter 7
Our Kill

It is many days later. A meat day. We are out on the grass-land. All of us except Dol. Dip is here too – we can't see him but we feel he is close.

Gak can smell a lion. It lies with its kill under some trees. Mab looks at her empty hands. It feels wrong that she has no brand. Sil smiles at her. "This time we'll let the lion keep its kill, Mab. Today we'll have our own kill."

It's hard to keep the Little Ones still and silent. And Wid. We need silence, because the meat we're after this time is alive and on swift hooves. We step through grass as tall as we are. I lead, with the Wid-thing in my hand and a bundle of sharp sticks at my belt. They all have flint tips.

Gak hisses. I turn. He is pointing. "That way," he whispers. "Deer." I nod and walk to where he is pointing. I pull a stick from my belt. The others follow, Wid last.

I spot the deer, a small herd is grazing by some rocks but they watch all the time. They keep lifting their heads to sniff the air. Today the breeze is blowing away from them to us and they can't smell us. I signal the others to stay, and creep forward alone. Each time an animal lifts its head, I stop. Even my breathing stops. Slowly, slowly I tip-toe closer. The stick is on the thong. It has a flint point at one end, and a tuft of stiff feathers at the other. I draw back the thong, the Wid-thing bends. There is power in that bend. It will hurl the stick from me to the animal – further than anyone could throw a spear.

I am close to the first deer. I daren't move, daren't breathe. I bend the Wid-thing as far as it will go, look along the stick to check it's pointed right and wait for the animal to lift its head.

It does, and sees me. It tenses. In an instant it will whirl and flee. I let go of the thong. The stick flies out. It flashes towards the deer and hits it with a thud. The point goes in. The deer bleats, snorts, shakes its head from side to side. Then it leaps away, my stick in its neck.

I turn. "Quick!" I cry. "It's hit, there's blood, it won't go far." I run after the fleeing herd, trying to follow the deer that's hurt. Mab and the others come behind, shouting and screaming.

The deer goes crashing through the high grass, leaving blood smears on stems. I can't see the animal but I can see grass rocking where it passes. Gak catches up with me. "It's bleeding a lot," he pants. "It must grow weak."

We race on, and almost fall over the animal. It has stopped, with its legs splayed out and its sides pumping. A ribbon of blood stains its coat from neck to foreleg. The stick has snapped off, there's just a stump sticking out. The animal's mouth lolls open, pink foam glistens on its nose.

Everyone has caught up. "Poor zebra," croons Wid. The Little Ones laugh. "It's a deer," whoops Bub. Wid nods. "Poor deer."

As we watch, the deer's front legs fold up. It falls forward and topples onto its side where it lies, shivering. I bend down quickly and slit its throat. Then I spring up, push the Wid-thing at the sky and howl with joy. The others dance and whirl, grin and wave their spears. It's only a deer but it's our deer. Our *kill*.

Chapter 8
Lion Dance

Mab goes off at a run to tell Dol what we've done. Lom puts the deer over his back and sets off. I call Bub to me. "You won't be a Brand-man, Bub, or a Snatcher. Instead you'll learn to use this, and these." I hold out the Wid-thing and the sticks.

The boy grins. "Can I carry them home now, Tan?"

I grin too. "Why not?" I tuck the sticks down his belt and hand him the weapon. It is as tall as he is. He sets off after Lom. The rest of us follow. We laugh and sing.

As we walk uphill, we see Dol and Mab waiting. They smile to see Bub with the Wid-thing and the sticks. Lom has built up the fire. He is cutting the meat.

"Time for the Lion Dance," says Dol. She loves to sing and clash the stones. I shake my head.

"No lion today, Dol. This is *our* kill."

"I know." She smiles. "Mab told me the story. We have made a *new* Lion Dance." She has our lion skin over her arm. She turns towards Wid.

"Wid, come to me." The Fool brings his wet, empty smile to the Old One.

"Put this on." She holds out the skin.

Wid gawps at it, shakes his head. "Wid not lion, Dol. Wid zebra. Poor zebra."

Dol shakes the skin. "Put it *on*, Wid."

The others see what Dol's doing. They come round. Gak frowns at Dol. "The lion skin," he growls, "on the *Fool*?"

"Yes," says Dol. "Today, Wid is the lion."

Gak shakes his head. "A fool in a lion skin is still a fool," he mutters.

Dol calls little Bub, takes the weapon, shows it to Gak. "What is this, Gak?"

"Tan calls it the Wid-thing," says Gak softly.

"Why does he call it that, Gak?"

"Because Wid made a little one, for a game."

"Wid made the *first* one, Gak."

"For a *game*, Old One. He didn't know ..."

Dol shakes her head. "No Gak, he *didn't* know. His head is full of fur and feathers. But when he looked at us he saw we were like jackals. He wanted us to be lions. This ..." she shakes the weapon, "this makes us into lions. From today we can kill for ourselves, like lions. We don't have to be like jackals and steal our meat."

So Wid the Fool puts on the lion skin. Its head is on his head. The Wid-thing is in his hand. The sticks are stuck down his belt. The rest of us pretend to be the deer. The little ones are birds and mice and lizards. They squeak and wiggle their fingers. Dol sings a song of danger, but we are not afraid. We eat the grass. If the danger comes closer, we can run. Nothing runs faster than a deer.

The danger is closer. We look up. Time to run. Dol sings a swift song, full of leaping. We start to run. Nothing runs faster than a deer. But now Dol sings a new song, about how quickly the stick flies through the air. It is faster, much faster than we are. We are hit. We run, bleeding. Our speed bleeds out of us.

We fall. The danger is on us. Dol bleats and clashes the stones.

The Fool stands tall and lifts his arms to the sky. The lion's head is on his head, its snarl above his empty smile.

The dance is done. It is time to eat.

Barrington Stoke would like to thank all its readers for commenting on the manuscript before publication and in particular:

Joshua Black

Jenny Bullen

Mary Campbell

Zachary Campbell Dean

Andrew Jordan Dearling

Ella Carnel Jones

Matthew Dowson

Autumn Hockaday

William Fenton

Jake Fisher

Callum James

Jay Kind

Asher Knight

Alexandra Leeson

Alwyn Martin

Bethan McCullough

Georgie Redman

Tia Ruel

Chirag Shaw

Hayden Smallwood

Lauren Spencer

Ben Sturgess

Martisha Thompson

Danielle Wallace

Joel Waring

Imogen Whiting

Become a Consultant!

Would you like to give us feedback on our titles before they are published? Contact us at the email address below – we'd love to hear from you!

info@barringtonstoke.co.uk
www.barringtonstoke.co.uk

Knife-Edge

Cecil True's gang runs Sam's estate. They beat kids up, nick their stuff. Sam's scared he's next. That's why he steals the commando knife. When he carries the knife, Sam thinks he's safe. He thinks he's hard. He thinks he can take on Cecil True. Sam's wrong.

Burnout

One spark was all it took. He was hooked from the first flame. Now, when Josh starts fires, nothing else matters. It's just him. The moment. The power. But like they say, if you play with fire, someone's going to get burned ...

Snakebite

Snake in the grass ...
Mark is the boss on the
estate. He thinks Alex
grassed him up. Mark isn't
happy.
Now Alex is hunted,
trapped – and on his own.
After all, Mark is the boss,
and Alex is a loser with
only a pet snake to talk to.
Get out of that one, Snake
Boy ...

Snapshot

Click. That's how easy it is.
To take a photo. To change
your life.
Victor didn't mean to get
involved. But what if, before
you know it, you've taken
photos of a crime? And now
someone wants those
photos back. *Bad.*
Can Victor manage to stay
alive?

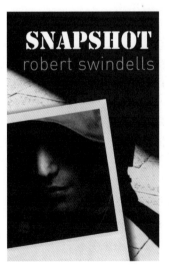

You can order these books directly from our website at
www.barringtonstoke.co.uk